GLORIA
Goes For GOLD

For my little brother
William, with love. A.T. xx

OXFORD
UNIVERSITY PRESS

Great Clarendon Street, Oxford OX2 6DP

Oxford University Press is a department of the University of Oxford.
It furthers the University's objective of excellence in research, scholarship,
and education by publishing worldwide. Oxford is a registered trade mark
of Oxford University Press in the UK and in certain other countries

Text © Oxford University Press 2024
Illustration © Annabel Tempest 2024

The moral rights of the author and artist have been asserted

Database right Oxford University Press (maker)

First published 2024

British Library Cataloguing in Publication Data available

ISBN: 978-1-38-205159-0

1 3 5 7 9 10 8 6 4 2

Printed in China

The manufacturing process conforms to the
environmental regulations of the country of origin

FSC
www.fsc.org

MIX
Paper | Supporting
responsible forestry
FSC® C020056

'Oi, what's going on up there?' Gloria yelled.
Monkey swung down from the treetops and landed with a twirl.

'I'm sorry!' he said. 'I was
doing my gymnastics training.
I didn't see you down here.'

'That's ok,' Gloria replied. 'Gymnastics sounds like swirly, twirly fun.
Could you show me how to do it?'

So Monkey trained Gloria for the balance beam event:

'Arch your back . . . beautiful!

Point your toes . . . tremendous!'

Gloria loved swirling and twirling, twisting and turning.
But she did NOT love stumbling or tumbling and landing with a **THUD**!

'It's a shame you don't have a tail to help you balance,' said Monkey.

'My bottom hurts!' Gloria groaned.
'It's much nicer to land with a SPLASH in the water.

Gymnastics is not for me.'

Gloria decided to cool off her bruised bottom while she chose a different sport. She plodded to the lake, jumped into the water, and . . .

wallop!

Crocodile swam nose first into Gloria's backside!

Marina Firth

Annabel Tempest

GLORIA
Goes For GOLD

OXFORD

UNIVERSITY PRESS

Gloria loved **WINNING**. She was part of her family's
synchronised swimming team.

They were gifted . . .

graceful . . .

even groovy . . .

and they **ALWAYS** won gold
at the Artistic Swimming Championships.

Her family had collected walls of awards, piles of plaques, and towers of trophies. But Gloria dreamt of a prize she didn't have to share.

And her chance arrived in the morning post . . .

'The Savannah Games are coming to town!'
bellowed her brother Harold.
'We need to rehearse our routine!'

Gloria had other ideas.

'This is it!' she thought. 'My big break!
I'll try a sport I can win all by myself.'

As her family splish-splosh-splashed
into the water, Gloria marched
off in the other direction.

Gloria spotted Cheetah training for the 200-metre sprint. Cheetah zipped one way, zapped the other, then suddenly she was zooming right towards Gloria!

CRASH!

'You should look where you're going,' huffed Gloria.

'I'm sorry!' Cheetah said. 'I was sprinting so fast I didn't see you!'

'Sprinting does look like fun,' replied Gloria,
thinking she could zip and zoom as fast as Cheetah.

'I'd like to give it a try!'

Cheetah beamed. 'Great idea! I can be your coach!'

So Cheetah showed Gloria how to run like a champion:
'Swing your arms and you'll go superfast!
Breathe with your belly.'

'And my top-secret
sprinting tip?
BE A CHEETAH!'

'Thanks, coach!'

At first, Gloria had fun zipping
and zooming around.

But after a while, things didn't feel right.

Sprinting wasn't swirly or twirly,
like artistic swimming.

It was a bit too straight for Gloria.

'I think I need to find a sport
with more pizazz!' she thought.

Gloria plonked down under a shady tree, wondering which sport to try next. A little leaf floated down and landed on her nose . . . then another. . . then **HUNDREDS** of them!

'YOWZER!'

yelled Gloria.

'I'm sorry!' Crocodile said. 'I'm training
for the 800-metre swim. I didn't see you!'

'That's ok,' said Gloria, 'I'm a *wonderful* swimmer!
I'd love to train for the swimming race.'

'I can give you some pointers, I guess,' said Crocodile.

So Crocodile trained Gloria.

'Curve your arms!'

'Go faster!'

Gloria loved sploshing and splashing in the water.
But as she swam back and forth, she realised
that there was still one problem.

She was lonely.

Gloria wondered if winning a medal of her own
was really such a great idea. 'I miss my family,' she thought sadly.

Back at the pool, Gloria's family
were practising their routine.
Gloria watched as a wobbly Harold
took her place in their special lift.

'I wish I could join in,' Gloria sighed.
'But they'll be so disappointed that
I ran off like that.'

So instead, she stayed in the bushes
and watched them sadly.

The next day was the start of the Savannah Games.
Gloria hid in the crowd to watch the artistic
swimming. 'The least I can do is cheer
my family on,' she thought.

The flamingos were fantastic. The buffalos were brilliant.
Then Gloria's family lined up, waiting for the whistle to blow.
Harold looked worried.

'I can't do it, Jemima,' Gloria heard him whisper.
'We have to try our best,' her cousin, Jemima, whispered back.

Then the whistle blew and into the water they dove.

Gloria watched from the edge of her seat. Harold was very shaky.
Each lift got WOBBLIER and WOBBLIER.

Gloria knew their last lift was coming up,
and it was the trickiest of all.
'I need to help them!' she thought.

The countdown was on!
Gloria knew she had 10 seconds before the final lift.

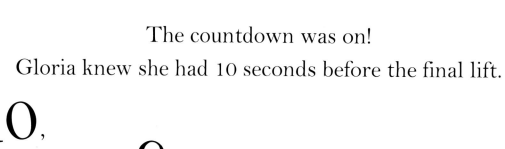

10,

9,

8 . . . Gloria sprinted to
the edge of the water.

7,

6,

5 . . . She dove in, and
swam as fast as she could.

4, 3, 2 . . . Harold gave Gloria a toothy grin when he saw her coming . . .

1

SPLISH, SPLOSH, SPLASH!

Gloria swooshed to take her usual place in the lift, and Harold flew over her with his arms spread wide. It was sensational!

Gloria's team was too wobbly to win gold . . . but they won the bronze medal! When they took their spot on the podium, the crowd whooped and cheered.

Hurrah!

MOOO!!

YIPPEE!

1st

2nd

'I'm sorry I missed training,' Gloria said.
Before she knew it, her family crammed around
her in an enormous hippo hug.

'We forgive you!' they cheered.
'And thank you for saving me during that lift,' whispered Harold.

Gloria grinned. Being part of this team was the best prize of all.